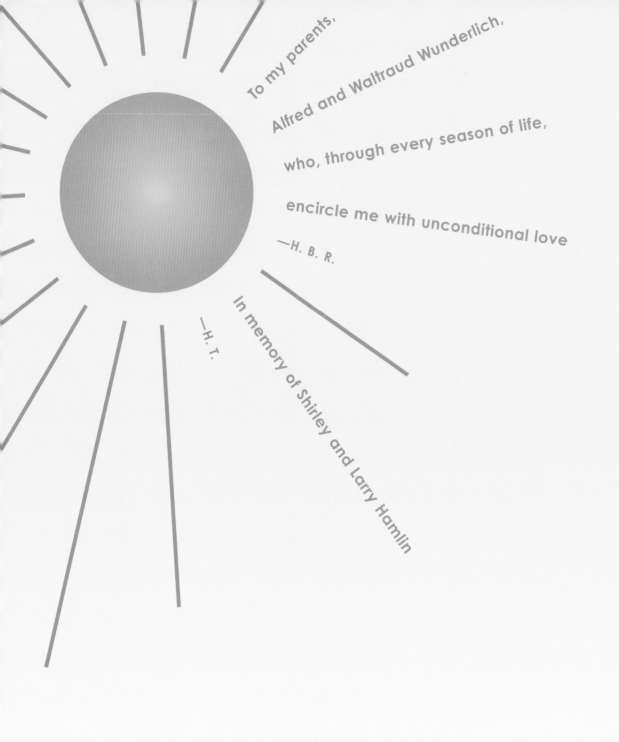

To my parents,
Alfred and Waltraud Wunderlich,
who, through every season of life,
encircle me with unconditional love
—H. B. R.

In memory of Shirley and Larry Hamlin
—H. T.

COME TO MY

And Other Shape Poems

PARTY

WRITTEN BY

Heidi B. Roemer

ILLUSTRATED BY

Hideko Takahashi

HENRY HOLT AND COMPANY • NEW YORK

Contents

Spring

Summer

Autumn

Winter

Spring

Jump-Rope Jingle

She jumps barefoot, I wear socks; Spring's the new kid on the block! Lock her up and toss the key; Springtime, say you'll stay with me!

Dainty Lady

Every day Miss Ladybug wears her very best. Doesn't she look dandy in her polka-dotted dress?

It's Raining!

Pitter patter

Plip plop!

Rain falls

from the sky...

I open my umbrella up

and I stay dry

The Happy Gardener

I
take
my
little
rake
and
my
hoe,
hoe,
hoe;

And
break
up
clods
of
dirt
in
each
row,
row,
row.

I
scatter
tiny
seeds
as
I
sow,
sow,
sow;

With
water,
sun,
and
patience,
beans
will
grow,
grow,
grow!

Big Fat Caterpillar

Which end is his head? Which end is his bottom? Good grief! A hungry robin

ALMOST GOT HIM!

Home Tweet Home

Hello, Little Wren! Please be my guest.

Your eggs will be safe in my birdhouse nest.

Sing loud, Little Wren! Now, don't be shy.

Your chicks will hatch, and away

they'll

fly!

In the Nest

Snuggled in a cuddly nest,

awakened from their sleep

hungry nestlings stretch their beaks . . . .

. . . and peep peep peep!

Kite in Flight

String, be strong. I'm holding on. Don't snap or slip away. My kite flies high up in the sky—so, string, be strong today!

Come to My Party

Birthday party. Funny caps. Games and gifts. Bows and wraps. Birthday cake. Fancy dishes. Blow the candles . . . . Happy wishes!

Summer

Beach Buddies

By the splishy splashy ocean,

where we wiggly giggly play,

We build dandy sandy castles . . .

till they're wishy washed away!

Watermelon

A sliver, a slice, deliciously nice; a nibble, a dribble, a lick.

And when I'm done, I pucker my lips; I'm ready! I aim and I . . . spit!

18

Celebrate

It's a day for parades and for clowns who say "hi!"
For loud marching bands and balloons in the sky.
It's a flag-waving day! Here's a flag just for you.
Hooray for parades and the red, white, and blue!

We love parades.

19

Garden Hose

Garden hose dozes like a lazy snake. When I turn on the faucet— what a hissing it makes!

Dandelion

Summer snowflake
made of fluff
I pluck a wisp and gently puff.

Seeds drift off
on wayward routes—

like

tiny

tufted

parachutes.

Gone Fishin'

I sit beside a gurgling brook;
a wiggly worm upon my hook. . . .
I sit and sit and wait and wait.
Fishy, won't you take my bait?

Night Sparkle

Splintering, scattering, like stars that are shattering, dazzling fireworks flash.

Echoing, thundering, like cannonballs rumbling, fireworks...

crackle
and
crash!

Marshmallow Treat

fun,
fun,
fun.

Spear a 'mallow, spongy sweet;

done,
done,
done.

Hold stick over flame, and heat till it's

yum,
yum,
yum!

Eat the toasty, roasty treat;

24

Camper's Prayer

Starlight, shine bright on my little tent tonight. If it should rain, and skies turn bleak—I pray my tent won't spring a leak.

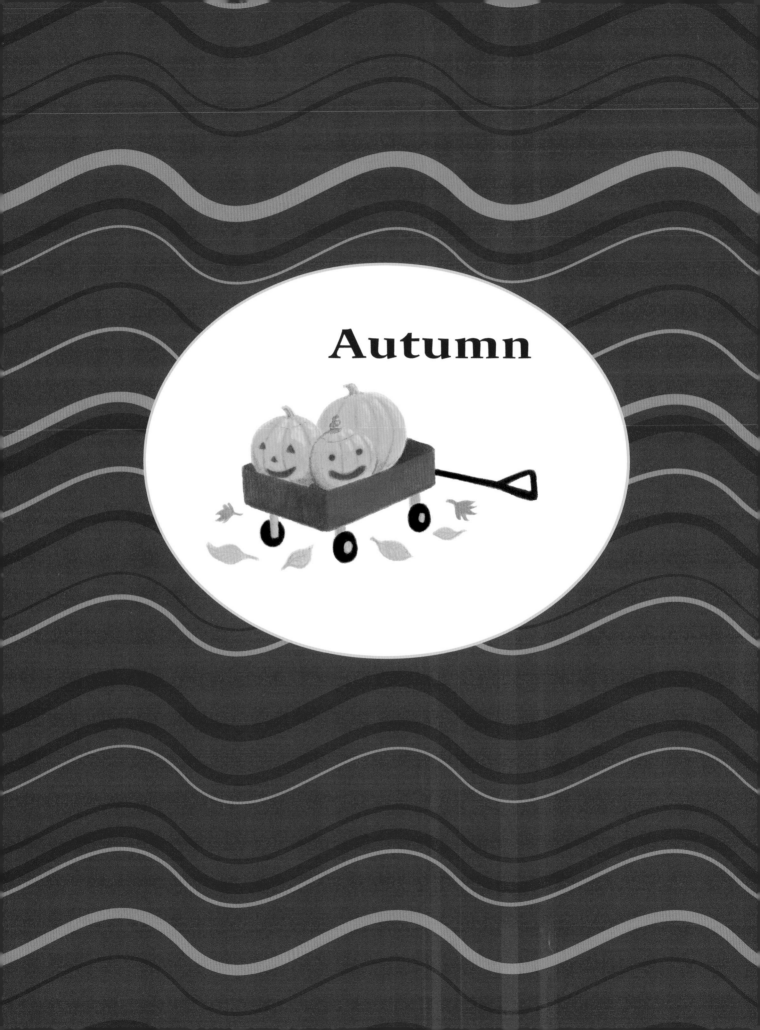

Autumn

Dancing Leaves

Crimson and coral and yellow as butter—

We reach up to snatch waltzing leaves as they flutter.

Hip, hip, hooray for fall's festive confetti!

Let's—

heap the leaves up and jump!

Are you ready?

The Spider

Dangling from her yo-yo string, Spiderling swings low.

I Like Crows

Like fat black clothespins perched in rows, cackling flocks of hungry crows cry "Caw! Caw! Caw!" from telephone poles.

Wheeee!

Mother taught her little daughter how to tip the teeter-totter.

Pumpkins for Sale

Rumple dimple dumplin' *pumpkin* patch!

Buy a perfect *pumpkin*—mix and match.

Riddle diddle rumpkin *pumpkin* spree.

Pick one you can carry . . .

and your *pumpkin* is free!

Harvest Slice

The Wishbone

Snap!

Thanks for food that tastes delicious, for helping hands to wash the dishes, for hide-and-seek and baby's kisses. Oh, happy day! So, who needs wishes?

Evening View

I hear their **V**oices o**v**erhead, a flock of geese in flight.

Geese form a **V**aliant letter **V**, then **V**anish from my sight.

Who's There?

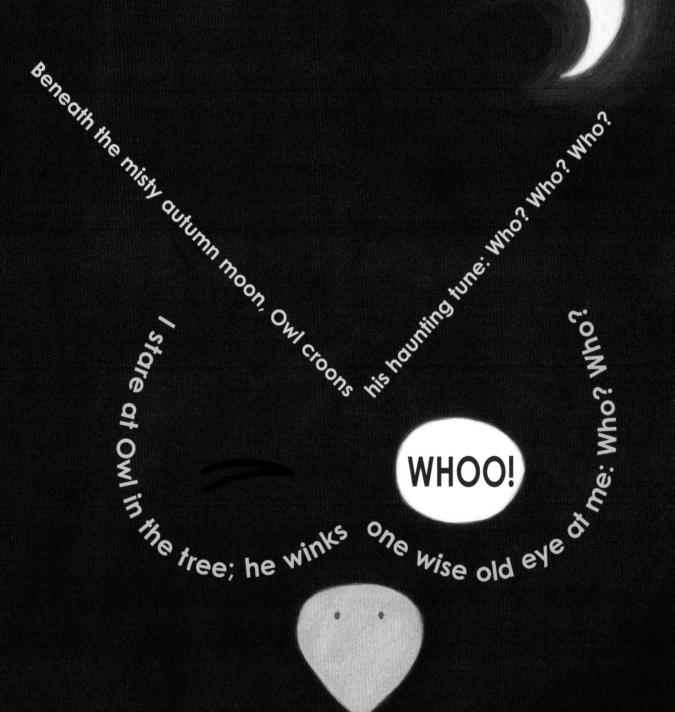

Beneath the misty autumn moon, Owl croons his haunting tune: Who? Who? Who?

I stare at Owl in the tree; he winks one wise old eye at me: Who? Who? Who?

WHOO!

Winter

My Big Hill

Tramping uphill through the snow, with my new red sled I go! Oh, what fun for you and me; slipping, sliding, sledding....WHE-E-E-E!

New Mittens

One mitten, two mittens, brand-new red-and-blue mittens.

Watch me build a snowman; see me clap, clap, clap!

Old Mittens

Green mittens, gold mittens; I just found these old mittens. . . . . . Gave them to my snowman. What a jolly old chap!

Special Delivery

Merrily, merrily,

Diddle dee dum!

Through the door my daddy comes,

Merrily, merrily, diddle dee dee!

He's bringing home our Christmas tree!

Happy Hanukkah

I watch my papa light the candles one by one. We'll all celebrate with gifts, games, music, food, and fun. Happy, happy Hanukkah, everyone!

Backyard Fun

Packing, stacking icy lumps; throwing, rolling snowy clumps.

Snowy walls and snowy floor; I wiggle through my igloo door.

Pickety Fence

Every slat of the **pickety fence** is crowned with a wintery cap;

I knock it off the **pickety fence** with a hippety clippety clap.

It's fun to strum the **pickety fence** with my ippety whippety whack;

I scurry to the end of the street and **pickety rickety** back.

43

Snowy Steps

HEAVE HO!
Shovel snow.

Yup, yup!
Scoop it up.

Dig deep.
Repeat.

What fun!
All done.

Uh-oh.
Wind blows.

Gusts shift,
big drift.

Dig deep.
Repeat.

Shovel snow.
HEAVE HO!

44

Icicles

Winter's
icy
fingers
grip
the

gutter's
numb
unsmiling
lip.

Bit by bit
the ice
spikes
slip
as

sunshine
shrinks
them
drip
by

d
r
i
p.

Mr. Moon

Mr. Moon's silhouette is milk-white and thin.
He hasn't a nose—just a forehead and a chin.

Good-bye, Winter!

I climb up a rainbow; I slide down a sunbeam; I glide on a breeze. "Good-bye, Winter!" I sing. I bounce on cloud pillows; I pounce on tall willows. Tomorrow is finally the first day of Spring!

Henry Holt and Company, LLC
Publishers since 1866
115 West 18th Street
New York, New York 10011
www.henryholt.com

Library of Congress
Cataloging-in-Publication Data
Roemer, Heidi B.
Come to my party and other shape poems /
Heidi B. Roemer; illustrated by Hideko Takahashi.
Summary: Poems that celebrate favorite things
from different seasons of the year, each shaped like
the subject at hand. 1. Size and shape—Juvenile
poetry. 2. Seasons—Juvenile poetry. 3. Children's
poetry, American. 4. Concrete poetry, American.
[1. Size—Poetry. 2. Shape—Poetry. 3. Seasons—
Poetry. 4. American poetry.]
I. Takahashi, Hideko, ill. II. Title.
PS3618.O37 C57 2004   811'.6—dc22
2003056568

ISBN 0-8050-6620-9 / First Edition—2004
Designed by Meredith Pratt and Donna Mark
Printed in the United States of America
on acid-free paper.
1 3 5 7 9 10 8 6 4 2

The artist used acrylics
on illustration board
to create the illustrations
for this book.